Bullets for Broadway

An Interactive Musical Comedy Mystery

Book and Lyrics by
David Landau

Music by
Killer Tracks

A SAMUEL FRENCH ACTING EDITION

RENTAL MATERIALS

An orchestration consisting of **Performance CDs with Vocal Backing Tracks** will be loaned two months prior to the production ONLY on the receipt of the Licensing Fee quoted for all performances, the rental fee and a refundable deposit.

Please contact Samuel French for perusal of the music materials as well as a performance license application.

IMPORTANT BILLING AND CREDIT
REQUIREMENTS

All producers of *BULLETS FOR BROADWAY must* give credit to the Author of the Play in all programs distributed in connection with performances of the Play, and in all instances in which the title of the Play appears for the purposes of advertising, publicizing or otherwise exploiting the Play and/ or a production. The name of the Author *must* appear on a separate line on which no other name appears, immediately following the title and *must* appear in size of type not less than fifty percent of the size of the title type.

BULLETS FOR BROADWAY first opened in at the Murder to Go Dinner Theater in Cedar Knolls, New Jersey in March 2002.. The performance was directed by David Landau. The cast was as follows:

BAXTER MALLENSTOCK . . . . Leo Hatem

ELI BLAINE . . . . Jim Folly

TONY ALTO . . . . Joseph Molino

TOFFEE ALTO . . . . Katherine Smizer

MIMI SHERATON . . . . Tina Zoganas

ABIGAIL MULDER . . . . Deborah Lichtenstein

INTRODUCTION

I invented the interactive mystery play back in the early 1980s as an attempt to mix environmental theater with audience involvement. My goal was to allow the audience to experience the story as if they were extras in a movie. The entire production, from script to props, direction to surroundings, was oriented towards encompassing the audience in the world of the mystery and not merely with the game of solving it. Mystery parlor games existed since the turn of the century. As theater, it is the story of the characters which must always take centerstage – a story of people who find themselves in desperate situations and are compelled to perform desperate acts. The comedy must come from the characters and not at their expense or that of the story.

It can become tempting for cast members to play for a laugh, but this seldom works. The audience laughs the most at things that are played straight – discovering the humor for themselves. Audiences identify and sympathize with characters that are real and seldom with caricatures. An actors approach to an interactive mystery should be no different than that taken to Shakespeare or any other theatrical work. Why is the character there, what are they thinking, why are they doing what they do and what do they want? The more real, the more the audience becomes involved in this new reality and the more both they and the performers will enjoy the experience. The audience itself is utilized by the performer, as a prop, a confident, another cast member. The audience is on stage with them.

In a true mystery there can be only one logical culprit, pointed out not only by the clues, but by the motivation, personality and situation that character finds himself/herself in. While there are a number of other likely suspects, this character is the inevitable guilty party. The mystery has been sown well when the average of correct guesses is 10-20%. By the end of the play, when all is revealed, the audience should sigh a collective "Of course, I should have thought of that!"

The interactive mystery play offers theater patrons, performers and producers many unique opportunities. The audience can be taken to the edge with suspense and then suddenly dropped into a humorous release of tension. The characters can become so real that they can reach out and touch the audience, literally. The theatrical fourth wall is placed behind the audience. If done correctly, the interactive play can be one of the most involving forms of theater possible.

David Landau

Creator of the first interactive mystery play, "*The Mystery Express*", Dec. 1982
Member of The Dramatists Guild and Mystery Writers of America

CHARACTERS

BAXTER MALLENSTOCK – Producer of the new Broadway musical, *The Mafia Queen.*

ELI BLAIN – Naïve composer/lyricist/book writer of the musical.

TONY ALTO – Gangster who is the sole backer of the musical.

TOFFEE ALTO – Gangster's wife who is the star of the musical.

ABIGAIL MULDER – FBI agent, under cover as a chorus girl, trying to build a case against Tony.

BERNIE BROADHURST – Pretentious actor who plays the "Tony" part in the musical and is having a affair with Toffee – using her for her money. (Same actor as **TONY**).

MIMI SHERATON – Wealthy patron of the arts, Broadway investor and gossip columnist.

THUG - same actor as **ELI**.

AUDIENCE

Members of the audience should play the following roles:
> The show's director
> Theater critics (mad-libs of reviews)
> Chorus girls
> Back up dancers (Toffee recruits them)
> Theater Investors

SETTING

It's opening night, the review party, where everyone is waiting for the reviews to come out. A newspaper on the tables has a headline "State's Witness on Money Laundering Missing" and a smaller article "'*Mafia Queen*' opens on the Great White Way, starring a Real Mafia Queen. Is it Biographical or just bad taste?"

Characters mingle with guests, recognizing them as producers, investors, critics, and other theater high society types.

The Stage Manager gives each table a "Mad-Lib" asking them to help write a review by picking words as requested – without knowing the sentences they fit into. They will be titled: *The Record, The News, The Post, The Ledger* and *The New York Times.* As there are only five reviews, the same review can be given to two tables next to each other so that the cast can pick which one is better, by looking at them during the food breaks. Stage Manager should note and tell the cast which tables have which reviews.

AUTHOR'S NOTES

PERFORMANCE SPACE

The following play was designed to be performed in a dining room, dinner theater, night club, theater-in-the-round, or a thrust stage where the acting area is level with the first row. The intention is to make the audience feel like they are actually in the location of the story. The performance is a sort of reverse theater in the round, with action performed around the circumference of the seating area, as well as down the aisles and in the center. The audience should be seated at tables, either dinner or cocktail. Tables could be added in font of the first row in the case of thrust or arena stages. Audience members can also be seated on stage.

SCENES & BREAKS

The script is formatted into four or five scenes running in length from 12 to 20 minutes. Between each scene is time to serve a course of a meal, serve drinks, or play music as desired. During these breaks characters mingle helping to establish character and reveal information to the audience in a one on one manner. The script can easily be adapted to eliminate some of these breaks. If this is the desire, black-outs should take place between scenes, with an intermission between either scenes 2 and 3 (if four scenes) or 3 and 4 (if five scenes). There should be some kind of break just before the finale scene to allow audience members to hand in their guesses as to "whodunit."

MUSICAL NUMBERS

The musical numbers in the show have been designed to be performed to recorded backing tracks. Once a license has been signed, a CD with recordings of both the instrumentals and the composer singing the lyrics can be obtained from Samuel French, Inc. Lead sheets will be provided when available. Also on the tape is the opening theme music which is to be used at the beginning of each scene.

AWARDING PRIZES

The "Sleuth Sheets" are handed out with the programs at the beginning of the night and collected by the characters before the finale scene. They should be handed to the Stage Manager, who will sort out the correct answers. After the curtain call, the correct answers are handed to the main character, who reads out the names of the successful sleuths. Generally, all correct answers are placed in a hat and a character draws one name. A prize is then awarded to that patron by a cast member. The prize can be a bottle of wine, a T-shirt, almost anything. It's the thought that counts.

PRE-SHOW MINGLES

BAXTER – Baxter moves from table to table, introducing himself and recognizing people as rich Broadway backers, reviewers or fellow producers. He reminds them of his past productions "Rats – now and forever in the alley behind the Winter Garden," "Move over *Titanic*, there's a new disaster in town: *Hindenberg – the Musical*," "*West Village Story* – a musical that's fun and gay," and of course "*Into The Hood* – an inner city fairytale." Now, with *The Mafia Queen* such a hit, he tells guests he is presently allowing only select investors the opportunity to get in on his next musical – "*Enron* – the musical," or: "*How Not to Succeed in Business Without Really Trying.*"

ELI – Shyly introduces himself to each table, asking if they liked the show and mentioning that he wrote it. He asks where everyone's from and tells them he's from Gary, Indiana. Ever since he saw *The Music Man* in grade school, he knew he wanted to become a playwright. He asks people what they do for a living, because he is looking for inspiration to write his next musical. He wrote *The Mafia Queen* by interviewing Toffee Alto – "She's a (whispered tones) gangster's wife. But don't tell anyone."

ABIGAIL – She introduces herself to the tables (acting like a dumb chorus girl). She asks guests if they know the show's producer Baxter Mallenstock or the show's backer, Tony Alto. She says she's heard that Mr. Alto is in organized crime. She asks people if they know what that means. She asks if anyone else here is in the same organization.

TOFFEE – She introduces herself to the tables. She thanks them for coming to see her show and remarks at how it was standing room only. "And did you hear all the applause?" "And they laughed at so many places we never thought we'd get a laugh. You know, like at places we thought were, like serious. But I guess that Eli really knows when to pull out a joke." She tells people how hard she worked for this show, even taking private acting lessons with her co-star, that famous Broadway idol Bernie Broadhurst the third. He helped her a lot.

TONY – Tony moves from table to table, telling everyone that they "enjoyed the show." He's not asking them, he's telling them. He put up the cash so his wife could star on Broadway. He knew a guy, who knew a guy, who Mallenstock owed money to. So he approached Mallenstock and made him an offer he couldn't refuse. The rest, as they say, is freakin' history. He recognizes a few people as owing money to him, and a few men as being regulars at his men's club Badda Bings, and a few women as being dancers from his club.

Scene One

(The characters are mingling. Lights dim out. Music begins. Lights up, everyone sings "Opening Night.")

EVERYONE.

IT'S OPENING NIGHT
SOON WE'LL BE READING ALL THE RE-VIEWS
OPENING NIGHT
EITHER WE WIN OR WE WILL LOSE
IT WAS A THRILL
ALL SEATS WERE FILLED

BAXTER.

EVEN THE CAST WAS ON TIME
CURTAIN WENT UP, THEN I UP-CHUCKED,
BUT NOW I THINK I'M DOING FINE.

EVERYONE.

IT'S OPENING NIGHT
SOON WE'LL BE READING ALL THE RE-VIEWS
WISH AS WE MIGHT
HEAR JUST PRAISE AND NOT SING THE BLUES
WHAT WILL THEY SAY?
BE YEA OR NAY?
THIS IS THE MO-MENT OF TRUTH
COULD THIS JUST BE IT?
THIS SEASONS BIG HIT?
OR A GOOSE?

*(Music under as **BAXTER** shakes hands with audience members.)*

BAXTER. Mr. Schubert, *(to another man)* Mr. Bialystock, so sorry I couldn't let you in on this great show. But, Mr. Tony Alto backed the entire thing himself. Mr. Alto?

*(**TONY & TOFFEE** join him.)*

BAXTER. *(cont.)* Tony, I'd like to introduce you to the two most famous names on the Great White Way.

TONY. What, their names are Moby and Dick?

TOFFEE. *(pulling him away)* What are you doing insulting the most famous theatrical producers of all time, you strunz!

(**ELI** *pulls* **BAXTER** *away.)*

ELI. I can't believe it. Opening night and a sold out house!

BAXTER. Yeah – and for only ten bucks a seat.

ELI. You sold the tickets for only ten dollars a piece?

BAXTER. Of course not, Eli. I went to the half price tickets line and gave everyone there ten bucks to come to our show. Packed the house like that *(snaps fingers).*

ELI. You – *(assuming he's joking)* you didn't! If you paid people to fill the seats, how did the box office take in so much cash. I walked by the box office window and there were bags and bags of green bills – big stuffed bags –

BAXTER. Shush – my naïve, creative friend. You just worry about writing us our next big show. After all, this room is filled with potential investors just waiting to be tapped.

ELI. But do you really think we'll get good reviews?

BAXTER. Good reviews? At ten thousand bucks a pop, we better.

ELI. Ten thousand a – what?!

(**BAXTER** *laughs at* **ELI** *and puts his arm on his shoulder as they sing [the music comes back up]. Everyone sings.)*

ALL.
> IT'S OPENING NIGHT
> SOON WE'LL BE READING ALL THE RE-VIEWS
> OH WHAT A NIGHT
> IT'S SO HARD BE-ING IN OUR SHOES

ELI.
> A FEW FLUBBED LINES

CAST.
> THAT'S NOT A CRIME

ALL.

'SIDES THAT THE SHOW WENT JUST FINE
THE CURTAIN ROSE, THE WHOLE CAST FROZE,
THE SHOW STILL ENDED RIGHT ON TIME

IT'S OPENING NIGHT
SOON WE'LL BE READING ALL THE RE-VIEWS
OH WHAT A FRIGHT
HOPE WE GET ON-LY THE BEST NEWS

CAST.

COULD LOSE OUR JOB

BAXTER.

UPSET THE MOB

BAXTER & ELI.

WE CAN'T GIVE BACK ALL THE CASH

ALL.

HOPE IT'S A BIG HIT

BAXTER.

OR I'LL BE THE NEXT HIT

BAXTER.	**CAST.**
KER-SPLAT!	THAT'S THAT!

(Lights dim, spotlight stays on **BAXTER**. *He turns sideways. There is a photo-flash.)*

VOICE. Turn front.

*(***BAXTER*** turns front, holding a number under his chin. There is another photoflash.)*

You have one phone call.

BAXTER. Take a message! *(to audience)* Okay, I bet you're asking yourself, how did Baxter Mallenstock go from hit Broadway producer to felon in one evening. Well, – it was easy. Let me tell you about it.

(Lights come up. Characters are mingling, chatting, in pantomime as **BAXTER** *walks around and "introduces" each of them to the audience.)*

BAXTER. Of course, it might help if you knew some of the main characters in our little comic-tragedy. First there's my partner in this business of bright lights and lost fortunes, Eli Blaine. Eli is a playwright. That's someone with absolutely no social life, so they create their own and stick it on paper.

(He taps **ELI** *on the shoulder.* **ELI** *spins around to talk to him, excited.)*

ELI. Baxter – this is incredible. I've never been in a room with this many people before. And some of them even know my name.

BAXTER. Of course they know your name Eli. You're the playwright. You're the genius that created this fabulous success.

ELI. Thank you, Baxter. But – well – *(stage whisper)* you made me churn it out so fast – in only one month – that, it's really just not that good.

BAXTER. Good? *(laugh, slapping* **ELI** *on the back)* Why, Eli – I never said it was good.

ELI. But, you just – Didn't you just say –

BAXTER. I said it was a success. In show business, there's no relation been good and successful. They aren't even distant cousins. Sometimes they may accidentally bump into each other on a dark and stormy night, but in general, they pass on the street barely recognizing one another. Our next play, Eli – you can spend the time making that good. I'll give you a month and two weeks. Just make sure it's commercial. Now, go, Eli, and flirt with the chorus girls.

(He turns to leave, but turns back to **BAXTER** *before* **BAXTER** *can renew talking to the audience.)*

ELI. The chorus girls? They'll ignore me. Women always ignore me.

BAXTER. Not any more, my timid friend. You are Eli Blaine – composer, lyricist, book writer of a hit Broadway musical. Sure, those beautiful dancers may have done the mambo with the producer, the director, and the producer again, just to get the part. But now that the shows a success, they'll even mambo with the writer. Come on, I'll introduce you.

(BAXTER takes ELI to a table of women.)

Hello, ladies. Allow me to introduce the man that made it all possible, the author of our fabulous show who is eagerly working on his next Broadway hit, Eli Blaine, our playwright and my partner. Eli, allow me to introduce you to our chorus line's first string. – This is Bubbles, Bambi, Bunny, and *(pointing to a man)* Boom-Boom.

ELI. A pleasure. But what – ah – unusual names.

BAXTER. Yes, well, they learned dancing at the Doll House A Go Go school of choreography, an establishment owned by our primary backer. And I must say, ladies, I have never seen anyone do such a fine dance number with brass poles on a Broadway stage before. Just do me a favor *(turning to a women patron)* tomorrow night, when the number ends, don't stand on the edge of the stage and ask the front row for one dollar bills. Eli, I leave you to your adoringly easy public. *(pulls a few singles from his pocket)* And here, these might help.

(BAXTER hands him the bills, pats his shoulder and steps away. He talks to the audience.)

Eli really is a good playwright, although you'd never guess it from this show. I met him when he was the manager of my favorite fine dining establishment – the hotdog cart on the corner of Broadway and 42th street. One day he wrapped my sauerkraut in a page of his play. The rest, as they say, is history.

(BAXTER walks to TOFFEE, who has her back turned – as if talking to a table.)

BAXTER. *(cont.)* Next, there is the star of our show, Mrs. Toffee Alto. I know, I know, you're thinking the only reason she got the part was because her husband put up the cash – well – duh! Of course! That's how the theater business has been run for centuries. Who am I to change it?

(He taps **TOFFEE** *on the shoulder. She turns to him, excited.)*

TOFFEE. Oh, Baxter, Baxter, Baxter. Isn't this a dream come true? What an opening! What a show! They all loved me.

BAXTER. And who won't, my sweet Toffee. You stick in their teeth like salt water candy, so they can chew and savor you again and again. A star is born.

TOFFEE. Me? But I'm just a simple Jersey girl.

BAXTER. So was Meryl Streep, so was Whitney Houston, so was Lorraina Bobbet!

TOFFEE. Lorraina Bobbet? Wasn't she the gal that cut off her husband's –

BAXTER. Now you, Toffee Alto, will take your place in that list.

TOFFEE. Do I have to be after Lorraina Bobbet?

BAXTER. We'll put you in before her. Besides, it's her turn to be cut short.

TOFFEE. Oh, Baxter, you're so good to me. Everyone's been so good to me. What did I ever do to deserve all this!

BAXTER. You married a gangster.

TOFFEE. *(She laughs, thinking he's joking.)* Tell me honestly, Baxter – was I good? I mean, was I really good?

BAXTER. You were – *(thinking)* – like no one else!

TOFFEE. Oh, I was, wasn't I?

BAXTER. Oh, yeah. Like that moment at the beginning of the first act, when you first made your entrance, and didn't say a word for five whole minutes.

TOFFEE. I don't think anyone noticed.

BAXTER. No, I'm sure they thought you were supposed to just stand there staring straight out at them, frozen on the edge of the stage, while the orchestra kept playing the same opening stanza over, and over, and over –

TOFFEE. It was just it was the first time there was ever anyone in the seats. I wanted to count them all. I had only gotten about half way when that freakin conductor hit me with his baton.

BAXTER. It just slipped out of his fingers. I guess it got tired of doing the same swing back and forth over and over again.

TOFFEE. Yeah, well, he better not let that happen again. My husband's paying for those batons. Oh, Baxy – this is the most wonderful day of my life! I can't believe it! What did I ever do to deserve all this?

(She kisses him on the forehead and turns away.)

BAXTER. Married a mobster. Which brings us to our sole investor in the show, Mr. Tony Alto, a name familiar to everyone in the organized crime division of the tri-state area. A "legitimate" businessman with a lot of illegitimate income.

(He taps **TONY** *on the shoulder.* **TONY** *turns to talk to him.)*

(cliched, ethnic Italian) Tony –

TONY. Mallenstock – Hey, that wasn't a bad show for a front. You almost made my wife looked talented. Tell me, how long does a show usually take to "officially" turn a profit?

BAXTER. Oh, depends. On Broadway, if it's a real hit, anywhere from ten months to a year.

TONY. Well, then, my friend – you are going to become famous. 'Cause you're gonna be the first Broadway producer to turn a profit in one freakin night.

*(***TONY*** *laughs, slapping* **BAXTER** *hard on the back.* **TONY** *pulls out two cigars.)*

BAXTER. Mr. Alto – don't you think that might look a little –

*(***TONY*** *shoves a cigar into* **BAXTER**'s *mouth.)*

TONY. What?

BAXTER. *(with cigar in his mouth)* Well, just a tiny bit – suspicious?

*(***TONY*** *pulls* ***BAXTER****'s cigar out of his mouth.)*

TONY. It's a freakin sold out show! Every seat was filled! No one can argue with that!

BAXTER. Without a doubt, Mr. Alto. Without a doubt. But – ah – it's just not mathematically possible, even selling every seat in the theater, to recoup two million dollars in a single night!

TONY. Why not?

BAXTER. The new math!

TONY. Listen, Mallenstock, freakin' movies – like that Hairy Porter thing and that Tit-tanic where everyone's swimmin with the ice cubes at the end, racked in over thirty mil on their first day.

BAXTER. Granted. But we only have one theater while movies open in many at the same time.

TONY. But we got more seats than any freakin' movie theater.

BAXTER. But we only have one showing a night while movies have several a day.

TONY. So we add more showings. One in the morning, one at noon, after work, after dinner, then the midnight show. My kids love those freakin midnight movie shows – that Rocks of Horror thing.

BAXTER. Who'd come! The theater would be empty!

TONY. Hey, every ticket will be bought and paid for, on the books. If people just missed showing up for some reason – well – theater tickets are non-refundable, right?

BAXTER. Well, yes, of course – but to make the cast and orchestra show up –

TONY. You said the theater would be empty. Why would we have them show up? Use your head, Mallenstock. We'll turn a freakin profit by the end of the week and by the end of the month, we'll show quadruple the return on my investment, right?

BAXTER. Well – *(notices* **TONY**'s *glare)* absolutely right, Mr. Alto.

TONY. Freakin' right I'm right.

(**TONY** *slaps* **BAXTER** *on the back and pushes the cigar back into* **BAXTER**'s *mouth.* **TONY** *walks away.* **BAXTER** *continues to talk to the audience as* **TONY** *exits.)*

BAXTER. I would never disagree with Mr. Alto. He's our backer. And the last guy that disagreed with him ended up having a disagreement with an engineer – of a freight train while crossing the meadowlands. Not only does Tony Alto have deep pockets, but they're filled with brass knuckles and spare bullets. He did manage to get us some real sweetheart deals with the unions. But his interest in legit show business is strictly limited to showing that bags of mysterious cash are from a legit business.

So why am I, the great Baxter Mallenstock, theatrical producer extrodinaire, involved with this guy? Well, first there's the fact that I haven't had a square meal for months and I'm sleeping under my office desk. Why, I can't remember the last hit play I produced. Maybe that's because I've never produced a hit play. And when you've built up that kind of track record, investors don't come knocking. Only loan sharks *(slapping a male patron on the back)* and ex-wives *(handing a check to a female patron)* and I'm not sure which is scarier. You see, there's a catch in this business. You need to have a hit show to raise money for a hit show. And tonight, at long last, and with a little help – or should I say a lot of help – from the underside of New Jersey, Baxter Mallenstock finally has a hit Broadway opening.

And to help celebrate with the cast at the after show party were not only the gossip makers of the Great White Way, but also the theater worlds most promising potential investors. All with eager checkbooks and pens itching to write my name after "pay to the order of." Getting the financing for my next play would be as easy as – a desperate actress.

(turning to a female patron)

BAXTER. So, how badly do you *really* want to get into show business?

(Suddenly, **BERNIE** *makes his grand entrance, dressed in a smoking jacket, scarf and sunglasses, a drink already in his hand. On his arm is* **MIMI SHERATON**.*)*

BERNIE. Alright – we're here. Now the party can really begin!

BAXTER. Well, if it isn't beauty and the beast.

BERNIE. *(to* **MIMI***)* You beast.

*(***MIMI** *fake laughs.* **TOFFEE** *dashes up to* **BERNIE** *and the three exchange "air" kisses.)*

BAXTER. *(to audience)* And that is perhaps the most pompous lead Broadway actor in musical history – Bernard Broadhurst, the third – Broadway Bernie to friend and foe alike, and God help the producer that's fool enough to have him in their play. *(looking up, praying)* Oh, God, Help me! Help me! Help me!

*(***BERNIE** *walks up to* **BAXTER**, *leaving* **TOFFEE** *and* **MIMI** *to whisper.)*

BERNIE. *(throwing arm around his shoulder)* Baxter, Baxter, Baxter – I was wonderful tonight. I felt it, tonight! I was centered tonight! I was human tonight! I was –

BAXTER. Not yourself tonight!

BERNIE. I know you love me, Baxy – I saved your play! If I hadn't agreed to help coach Little Miss Mafia over there, even her husband would have pulled the money out. Either that, or he would have just lined us all up against some garage wall, like in Chicago and – well – it's just too exciting to think about.

BAXTER. Bernie, you are a conundrum.

BERNIE. Ooooo – Baxy, I never knew you cared.

BAXTER. One moment you're waltzing around with three dreamgirls from the chorus line on your arms and then next, it's three Jersey boys.

BERNIE. You know what they say, Life is a Cabaret. One should never limit where one gets ones inspiration. Take Mimi for instance.

BAXTER. No – you take Mimi.

BERNIE. Oh, I have, many times.

(**BAXTER** *puts the cigar in his mouth.* **BERNIE** *takes it out.*)

BERNIE. Ugh. Remember, you never know where it's been. Remember Monica? *(taking a drink from a near by table)* Are you going to finish that?

(As **BERNIE** *takes the drink and finishes it,* **BAXTER** *turns to the audience.)*

BAXTER. *(to audience)* We only cast Bernie because some people think he looks a lot like Tony Alto, which is the character he plays in the show, although personally, I don't see it. The gypsy he dragged in with him was none other than Mimi Sheraton – the number one gossip columnist of Broadway, a patron of the arts and a royal –

(**MIMI** *walks up.*)

MIMI. Baxter, Darling – what a play – what a night – what a waste of talent – the cast's darling, not yours. You have no talent to waste.

BAXTER. I'm crazy for you too, Mimi.

MIMI. Of course you are. Everyone likes to grease Mimi Sheraton. My column can make or break a show. I need a drink. A dry martini.

BAXTER. You're never dry, Mimi.

MIMI. Of course I am – after my bath, when I have the pool boy pat me down. *(She pats a man in the audience.)* And he always does such a good job. I even loaned him to my friend here, as a Christmas present. *(to the woman with him)* Tell me, has been naughty or nice? *(Who knows what she'll say.)* Oh, Bernie, dear, could you be a doll and fetch Mimi a little ittsy bittsy dry martini? If I don't have one in ten seconds, I'll be so le miserable.

BERNIE. Of course, my one and only. Do you like to it shaken or stirred?

MIMI. Surprise me.

(They growl at each other. **BERNIE** *exits to bar.)*

MIMI. *(to* **BAXTER***)* I just love a man who knows how to come back for more.

BERNIE. Mimi – you just love a man who –

MIMI. *(quickly interrupting)* So, Baxter, darling, how on earth did a man of your low caliber ever fool someone in to putting up two million for a show? Oh, that's right, his wife wanted to make her Broadway debut. Still, there must be other producers, with much more experience and talent, that would stoop that low. As a matter of fact, I don't think there's any producer who wouldn't stoop that low. So how did Tony Alto get stuck with you?

BAXTER. Mimi, you are always a breath of fresh air – right off a manure heap.

*(***ABIGAIL*** rushes in with a few newspapers as* **BERNIE** *returns with two drinks.)*

ABIGAIL. It's here! It's here! The first review is out.

(Everyone crowds around her. She hands out papers.)

BAXTER. *(to audience)* And that's Abigail, the only chorus girl our backer didn't personally hire – and the only one that can actually sing. She's from Oklahoma and some day she's gonna make some man a most happy fellow.

ELI. *(getting very close to her)* Which paper, Abigail?

ABIGAIL. *The Post.*

MIMI. Well, Baxter, looks like its time to see if you're going to be hearing the sound of music or coming down with a Saturday night fever. Oh, and look, the reviewer from the paper is even here tonight! Why don't we have him/her read their own work – aloud?

ELI. Maybe you could help read them, Abigail. You have such a heavenly voice – er – ah, it might soften the blow.

ABIGAIL. Well, alright. I'll read with them.

(**MIMI** *goes to the table with The Post mad-lib and selects someone to stand. The patron will read off the words from the list the table made, filling in the blanks as* **ABIGAIL** *reads the review.*)

TOFFEE. Was that a good or a bad review?

MIMI. Not every review is going to be a nine. Just be thankful you haven't gotten sunk like the Titanic yet. So far, you're still footloose and fancy free. But soon you'll be going deeper into the woods. The toughest critics are yet to come, so watch out. *(holding out her empty glass)* Bernie, darling, my glass is empty!

TOFFEE. *(holding up her glass)* Bernie, dear, I waited all this time to toast the opening of our show with you.

(**BERNIE,** *holding his own glass, looks back and forth between the women, who glare at each other.*)

ABIGAIL. *(to* **ELI**) Oh, I can't wait to see how he's going to get out of this one.

(**BERNIE** *pours part of his drink into* **MIMI***'s glass, then walks over to* **TOFFEE** *and raises his glass to hers.*)

BERNIE. To the Mafia Queen!

ALL. *(lifting their glasses)* To the Mafia Queen!

(As they start to drink –)

MIMI. And all who sail in her. *(She downs the glass.)*

(Black out. Mingle.)

PRE-SCENE 2 MINGLE

BERNIE – Introduces himself to all the tables, flirting with the women, telling them that he gives exciting private acting lessons. He talks about all the shows he's been in *Titanic* - he was the understudy for the iceberg, *Phantom* – he was one of people that dies, *Jekyll & Hyde* - he was one of the people that dies, *Civil War* - he was one of the people that dies. He's toured as one of the leads in the musical *Frankenstein* – what a monster of a show that was. "Well, enough about my career, lets talk about me."

MIMI – Introduces herself to the tables, flirting with all the men, telling them that she gives private Manhattan tours – the drink not the island, darling. She knows they are all fans of her column – who isn't. She just hated the show *The Mafia Queen* and can't believe her good friend Bernie agreed to be in it. But then, he is always desperate for money. "But then again, who isn't? (laugh)." She can't believe that Toffee Alto – what a no talent. She talks about all the affairs she's had with famous men, but won't mention their names. You remember that Senator from, you know. And there was that New York real estate tycoon who dropped his second wife for her – he got tired of blonds. And then there was that famous Russian ballet dancer – she showed him a few steps.

TOFFEE – She hates Mimi. She tells people Mimi is a leech, that clings onto poor Bernie. She won't let him go and doesn't know when she's lost. She kept showing up at rehearsals, throwing everyone off. She adores – I mean admires, Bernie. What a talent. He's been so wonderful and she never could have gotten through all the pressure with out his help and support. Her husband doesn't understand her like Bernie does. Maybe that's because he's another creative type like her.

ABIGAIL – She tells people that the shows backer, Mr. Alto, makes her nervous. He's very intimidating. She knows that he put up the money and needs to look after it, but he seems to be the only one with the keys to the box office. She asks people if they may have overheard any conversations Tony may have had with Baxter.

ELI – He tells everyone what a wonderful guy Baxter is. He took him from selling hotdogs on the corner of 42nd street to being a Broadway Playwright. Baxter is his only friend since he's gotten off the bus in New York. He also tells people that he thinks Abby is the best chorus girl Broadway ever created. Isn't she dreamy? But, he's too nervous to talk to her. He asks people for their advice.

BAXTER – He confides that he was surprised that Toffee Alto wasn't a disaster on stage, although any actress put next to Bernie she would look like Betty Buckley. He's sure the next reviews will be great and he has the paperwork for the limited partnership for his next production all ready.

Scene Two

*(Just before the scene begins, **ABIGAIL** and **TOFFEE** recruit two men from the audience and take them out. Outside, all four are draped in fake minks and given blond "big Jersey hair" wigs to wear. The audience chorus girls are instructed on how to strut and told to imitate whatever **ABIGAIL** does, staying behind her. They should just hum along with the music, "which is easy" and when cued by **ABIGAIL** to sing "The Mafia Queen.")*

*(Black out. "Mafia Queen" music begins. Spotlight hits **TOFFEE**, singing "The Mafia Queen.")*

TOFFEE.
I WISHED TO BE ONE
A MAFIA QUEEN
A BLOND WHO AIN'T DUMB
A MAFIA QUEEN
I THOUGHT IT'D BE FUN
TO BE MORE RICH THAN MY FRIENDS
MEAN GETS ALL IN THE END
SO I SNAGGED A MADE MAN

I WORKED TO MAKE IT

*(**ABIGAIL** enters with "chorus girls.")*

ABIGAIL & CHORUS GIRLS.
THE MAFIA QUEEN
TOFFEE.
SO ME, THE RIGHT FIT
ABIGAIL & CHORUS GIRLS.
THE MAFIA QUEEN
ABIGAIL.
REFUSED TO BE A LOSER
TOFFEE.
MY TIME TO BE THE CHOOSER
ABIGAIL.
NO ONE CAN STOP HER
THIS MAFIA QUEEN TODAY!

TOFFEE. Come on girls – lets show them what we've got!

    (Music break as the "girls" do a dance number, lead by **TOFFEE,** *which looks a lot like a stripper number.)*

ABIGAIL.

    SHE IS WHAT YOU SEE

TOFFEE, ABIGAIL & CHORUS GIRLS.

    THE MAFIA QUEEN

TOFFEE.

    THEY WISH THEY WERE ME

TOFFEE, ABIGAIL & CHORUS GIRLS.

    THE MAFIA QUEEN

ABIGAIL.

    SHE DON'T CARE IT'S BLOOD MONEY

TOFFEE.

    YOU WISH YOU HAD IT, HONEY

ABIGAIL.

    NO ONE CAN TOP HER

TOFFEE & ABIGAIL.

    THIS QUEEN IS HERE TO STAY!

    (Lights out. **TOFFEE** *and* **ABIGAIL** *take wigs and minks from audience chorus girls and send them back to their seats. After applause ends, spot light up on* **BAXTER.** *)*

BAXTER. That was the show's big Act One finale. Okay, Okay, so the Scarlet Pimpernel it ain't – which gives you an idea why I slipped ten thousand greenbacks to every reviewer that showed up. And while everyone at the after show party was reminiscing about that number and how the entire audience stared wide eyed and open mouthed at the stage during it, no one seemed to notice a small encounter not far from the front door.

    (Lights up as a **THUG** *enters, dressed in leather jacket, cap and sunglasses, chewing on a toothpick and clutching a gun in his jacket pocket. He walks up to* **TOFFEE, ABIGAIL, MIMI,** *and* **BERNIE** *who are talking about the song "The Mafia Queen." The* **THUG** *pulls* **BERNIE** *aside.* **BAXTER** *has exited.)*

THUG. Psssst?

BERNIE. I beg your pardon.

THUG. I says, Psssst!

BERNIE. The restroom is out the door and to the left.

THUG. Is that where's you want I should put it?

BERNIE. It would probably be the most appropriate place, don't you agree?

THUG. I won't know, boss – if you says so.

(**THUG** *turns to exit as* **BERNIE** *turns back to the ladies – but then* **THUG** *turns around again.*)

Pssst again!

BERNIE. Now what?

THUG. Your wife was looking freakin' good up there on dat stage. I think yous might have a hit.

BERNIE. Ah – praise from the little people. Now my life is complete. It could only be improved by one small thing.

THUG. What's that?

BERNIE. If you would stop calling me "boss" and disappear.

THUG. Oh – right, boss – I mean – good plan.

(*They start to part.*)

(*puzzled*) The restroom?

BERNIE. Out the door and to the left.

THUG. Hey, it's your party.

BERNIE. Yes – it is, and you're invited – to leave.

THUG. Right – gotcha. And leave it in the restroom.

BERNIE. Go away.

(**BERNIE** *turns away as* **THUG** *exits.*)

TOFFEE. Oh, Bernie, dear, we were just having a disagreement as to which got the bigger reaction. The Mafia Queen or our love song.

(*They look into each other's eyes. The music "Me and You" begins.*)

MIMI. Oh, no – I feel something coming on! I think I'm gonna be sick all over again.

TOFFEE. *(love in her eyes for* **BERNIE***)* The audience was on the verge of tears.

MIMI. Who could blame them?

BERNIE. *(love in his eyes for* **TOFFEE***)* So was I.

MIMI. So was every non-deaf person within a six block radius.

(She downs her drink as the couple breaks into singing.)

TOFFEE.

ME AND YOU
AND YOU AND ME AND YOU
ME AND YOU
YOU AND ME AND ME AND YOU

(There is the sound of a gunshot from the lobby. Only **ABIGAIL** *wonders if she heard something. The couple keeps singing.)*

BERNIE.

YOU AND ME
AND ME AND YOU AND ME
YOU AND ME
ME AND YOU AND YOU AND ME

(Another two gunshots. **ABIGAIL** *and* **MIMI** *notice, puzzled.)*

TOFFEE & BERNIE.

YOU AND ME AND ME AND YOU

(Another three gunshots. **ABIGAIL** *starts towards the front door, putting her hand in her purse [for her gun].)*

ME AND YOU AND YOU AND ME
AND YOU AND ME AND –
ME AND YOU
AND YOU AND YOU AND ME
ME AND YOU
YOU AND ME AND ME AND I

*(**TOFFEE** and **BERNIE** embrace and kiss passionately.
Music ends abruptly.)*

MIMI. Bernie! The show is over. You don't have to act like
you like her now!

*(**ELI** comes in, looking nervous.)*

ABIGAIL. Eli – I thought I heard gun shots out there!

MIMI. Probably a music lover shooting her ears off.

(She indicates shooting herself, then goes off to the bar.)

ELI. I have to find Baxter.

ABIGAIL. Is something wrong, Eli?

*(**TOFFEE** and **BERNIE** stumble past them, kissing madly.
They kiss and fumble their way out the back door.)*

ELI. Wow. How dedicated you actors are. Always rehears-
ing.

ABIGAIL. Eli, when you came in here you looked worried
about something. Is anything wrong?

*(She touches his hand. He virtually melts and stares into
her eyes, almost in a dream state.)*

ELI. No – yes – well – I'm not sure.

ABIGAIL. Eli, are you feeling alright?

ELI. Heavenly.

ABIGAIL. What did you need to see Baxter about?

ELI. Oh – it's nothing really. Just – well, do you remember
that actor that played the kidnap victim in the show?
He was so authentic, struggle, desperation, that look
of fear on his face. *(He tries to imitate it.)* God, what an
actor – so real. Odd, I don't remember ever seeing
him at the rehearsals –

ABIGAIL. Eli, what about him?

ELI. Well, I guess he got carried away with the celebration.
He's sick in the men's room, red wine all over his shirt.
This nice man trying to help him – one of the stage
hands –

ABIGAIL. What makes you think he's a stage hand?

ELI. He was wearing gloves. You know that guy that always wears a baseball cap, sunglasses, and a leather jacket? I saw him backstage during the show. Though I've never seen him at rehearsal either.

(**ABIGAIL** *takes a newspaper off a table and shows* **ELI** *the photo of the missing witness.*)

ABIGAIL. Did he look like this?

ELI. Oh, no, I don't think so. He was wearing sunglasses and –

ABIGAIL. I'm sorry, Eli, I meant the guy with the red wine all over himself. Did he look like the person in this picture?

(*She takes his hand and hands him the paper. He sighs and just looks at her hand touching his.*)

Eli?

ELI. (*looking deep into her eyes*) Yes?

ABIGAIL. The picture. Does it look like the actor in the men's room who spilled the wine on his shirt?

ELI. Oh – (*looking at photo*) As a matter of fact –I don't know. I didn't really get a good look at him and, well, he wasn't smiling like in this picture. He was more like – (*He imitates a dead man's face.*)

ABIGAIL. (*facetious*) Thank you, Eli – that was most helpful.

ELI. Oh, anything for you, Abigail.

ABIGAIL. Now think, Eli. This is really important –

ELI. Oh – if it's important to you – its important to me. (*smiles at her*) You know you have the most perfect eyes?

ABIGAIL. Okay. I want you to remember, did the nice stage hand see you?

ELI. No. They were both in the bathroom stall. I was going to offer to help but –

ABIGAIL. Do you think he's still there?

ELI. Well, I don't know – I guess he could – You think I should go back and –

(**ABIGAIL** *pulls out a gun and starts to dash out.*)

ABIGAIL. Damn – it's a mens room. I need an escort.

(She comes back and drags **ELI** *out with her.)*

ELI. Gee, I know the lines are always bad for the ladies room, but –

(She pulls him out – just as **BAXTER** *and* **TONY** *enter from the back room.)*

TONY. – it's what I call reciprocity. I scratch your back, you scratch mine.

BAXTER. Yeah, but you had somebody scratched out in the men's room. Wasn't he in the show? As the kidnap victim? Funny I never noticed him at rehearsals.

TONY. *(laughing)* Funny! You're freakin' funny yourself Mallenstock.

BAXTER. *(bashful)* Well, I –

TONY. *(deadly serious)* I don't like funny. That guy in the men's room – and I still don't know how the freakin' way he ended up in the men's room – he was beginning to act funny.

BAXTER. I'm not funny. Never have been. I know he's only an actor and there are as many of them in New York as there are cockroaches, but how am I to explain this to the actors union? We need a new actor because the last guy did something funny and our backer doesn't like funny. – Oh, you didn't mind that the play is a musical comedy?

TONY. Hey, I like them freakin' funny plays – it's funny people. And as far as getting a replacement for him – forget about it! I'll get one, no problem. Why, I bet I can get a new one almost every night.

BAXTER. But, that would complicate the payroll and –

TONY. Mallenstock, I'll handle the books.

BAXTER. We have Arthur Anderson for that.

TONY. Same thing. I still want to know who told that stooge of mine to dump the dead weight in the men's room. He's gonna get it, badda bing! Anyhows, this is what I mean by reciprosity here. I handle the books, you keep my wife busy in this freakin' play. Where is she anyway?

*(**MIMI** approaches them.)*

MIMI. Mr. Alto? I'm so delighted to meet you. I'm Mimi Sheraton, the voice of Broadway – that's my column. I thought it might be fun to interview you. The behind the scenes man who made it all possible. Who is he really? Why did he do it?

TONY. And with whom.

MIMI. *(coming close to him)* Oh, Mr. Alto?

TONY. Tony. It's Tony to my friends. And you and I – I get the feeling that we are going to become intimate friends.

(He whispers something in her ear and then grabs her on the butt. She jumps.)

MIMI. I can tell this is going to be a very exciting interview. I'd say we should start right away, in the back room, except I saw your wife and her leading man go in there. They were practicing their love scene, I believe.

TONY. Really? With a freakin' actor? That's even worst than the priest! That's it. Maybe I should go back there and help them practice their death scenes.

*(**TONY** exits. **BAXTER** attempts to stop him, but its too late. He growls at **MIMI**, who just laughs.)*

MIMI. I can't miss this – it'll be the first good show of the night.

*(She dashes out the back door as **ELI** comes dashing in the front.)*

ELI. Baxter! Baxter –

BAXTER. *(annoyed)* Now what – I mean, what's bothering you my wonderful creative partner?

ELI. Are you being facetious?

BAXTER. I wouldn't even know how to spell it.

ELI. F–A–C –

BAXTER. We can work on my vocabulary skills later, teacher. But right now, something seems to be bothering you. And although I myself am in a state of virtual panic over recent developments that I would rather not go into until necessary, or the receipt of a subpoena, perhaps your dilemma may provide for me a quick reprise.

ELI. Baxter, I think your vocabulary skills have come a long way.

BAXTER. Credit the teacher.

ELI. Why, thank you, Baxter. You know, I often thought that I might try teaching if –

BAXTER. *(grabbing his lapels)* WHAT WAS IT YOU WANTED?

ELI. *(almost in tears)* You don't have to yell!

BAXTER. *(brushing him off)* I'm sorry, Eli. It's just that my nerves are frayed thinner than an investors promise.

ELI. Funny you should say that –

BAXTER. Funny? *(worried)* How funny – ha, ha funny or peculiar funny?

ELI. Well, funny as in *(thinking it over)* maybe funny as –

BAXTER. Forget I ever asked. Go on, Shakespeare. What is bothering you?

ELI. Our backer, Tony Alto. I think *(he looks around)* I think he's a gangster.

BAXTER. Noooo.

ELI. Yes! One of the chorus girls – I'm not sure if she really is a chorus girl – she looks like a chorus girl – *(dreamily)* she looks like more than a chorus girl – she looks like –

BAXTER. The main course!

ELI. The entire menu – for a week!

BAXTER. That would have to be Abigail.

ELI. Yes – Abigail. Oh, what a name. Abigail, Abigail. Don't you just love saying it?

BAXTER. Let me see – Abigail! I don't know *(to man in audience)* You say it.

*(Audience member says "Abigail." **BAXTER** has a few more men say it. He gets a chorus of "Abigail" going.)*

ELI. It's music to my ears.

BAXTER. Right. Now, before we were so rudely interrupted by these lecherous gentlemen – what about Abigail?

ELI. I think she's an FBI agent.

BAXTER. *(grabbing him by the lapels)* What do you mean "you think" she's an FBI agent?

ELI. I thought I was perfectly clear!

BAXTER. *(still holding him)* Perhaps I should have said – Why do you think she's an FBI agent?

ELI. Because she told me?

BAXTER. *(slowly releasing him)* Of course – bad things always come in such tempting packages.

ELI. Baxter, she thinks that Tony is a *(looks around)* –

BAXTER. Gangster –

ELI. Mafioso – and that he's using our play to launder money.

BAXTER. Eli – do you know what it means to launder money?

ELI. Well – no, not really – but it doesn't sound good.

BAXTER. Why doesn't it? Who wants dirty money lying around. Wouldn't it be better if it were clean money? We launder our clothes. Is that so horrible?

ELI. But she said something about us all going to jail.

BAXTER. On second thought, who cares how dirty our clothes are, so long as they aren't striped.

ELI. Actually, they have these bright orange jump suits for prisoners now –

BAXTER. Eli – are you a costume designer now?

ELI. What are we going to do?

BAXTER. We are going to think.

ELI. Right! *(to audience member)* What are we thinking about?

BAXTER. *(to audience member)* What are we thinking about? Better not ask you – this is a family show. Eli, my partner, friend, co-defendant – we are thinking about how to get ourselves out of this jam.

(spotlight on **BAXTER***)*

BAXTER. *(cont.)* *(to audience)* That was when everything started going round like a crazy carousel. First Mimi and Toffee came running out fighting like cats.

(They run out screaming and fighting.)

Then Tony clocked Bernie – sending him flying out like Peter Pan.

(Punch sound and **BERNIE** *flies out. Both women help him up. They face off and put out their arms for him. He looks between them, then runs to* **TOFFEE***.)*

MIMI. I've put up with your little hobbies long enough, Bernie. Lets face it, little Mrs. Mafia Queen – you're just an easy meal ticket.

*(***TOFFEE** *belts* **MIMI***.* **BERNIE** *laughs.* **MIMI** *belts* **BERNIE***, who screams and runs out, with* **MIMI** *right after him)*

No one uses Mimi Sheraton and lives to laugh about it.

(They pass the entering **ABIGAIL***, who has three newspapers. She tosses them to* **ELI** *and pulls her badge – showing it towards the back room.)*

ABIGAIL. Alright, Mr. Alto. Agent Annie Muller, FBI.

EVERYONE. Annie?

ABIGAIL. It's time we talked about the dead actor in the men's room. The one who was going to play a state's witness on court TV!

TOFFEE. He's gone crazy – out of control. You'll probably have to shoot him. Annie, get your gun.

*(***ABIGAIL** *pulls her gun and starts into the back room.* **ELI** *starts to follow her.)*

ABIGAIL. *(exiting)* Eli, stay back. I wouldn't want you to get hurt.

ELI. She loves me!

TOFFEE. Shoot first – Officer!

(**ELI** *stays back as* **ABIGAIL** *exits.* **TONY** *enters, holding* **MIMI** *hostage.*)

TONY. I heard that, Toffee.

MIMI. *(loving it)* Oh, Mr. Alto, you're so rough – a regular Jekyll and Hyde. Tie me up!

TONY. *(sweetly to her)* It's Tony.

(*He whispers in her ear again.*)

MIMI. Oh – Tony.

TOFFEE. "Oh, Tony" What, she's jumping on your bandwagon too? Why don't the two of you just get a freakin' room at the Grand Hotel? Where's that FBI agent? I need her gun!

TONY. I bet it was you settin' me up by having that stiff dumped in the men's room. Well, I got it all figured out now!

TOFFEE. Yeah, I've got it all figured out too! You don't think I know what you've been doing with all those hand picked chorus girls of yours? You think I'm *stunada**? I bet they're all running off to Bernie too, 'cause unlike you, he's got a real big gun.

TONY. *(pointing gun at her)* You're asking for it, Toffee!

TOFFEE. *(grabbing silverware from a table)* Promises, promises!

(**ABIGAIL** *comes back in, gun aimed at* **TONY.**)

ABIGAIL. Alright, Alto! Drop the gun!

TONY. Take your farewell bow, Abigail, or Annie, or whatever your freakin' name is this hour. No dumb broads are going to double cross me.

MIMI. *(scared, realizing she's in the cross-fire)* Stop the world, I want to get off!

(*Everyone freezes.*)

BAXTER. *(to audience)* And it was at that tense moment that my partner did the most amazing thing – and proved himself to be a true theater trooper.

---

* (Italian. Translation: "Stupid")

ELI. *(looking at papers)* Hey – these reviews aren't bad! Doesn't anyone want to hear them?

(Everyone turns to look at him.)

BAXTER. I do, I do.

ELI. *(nervously trying to distract everyone)* Here's the review from *The News.*

*(Everybody stares at **ELI** as he dashes to a table and has them help him read the review [using their mad-lib].)*

MIMI. Now that's what I call sweet charity.

ELI. And here's the one from *The Post.*

*(**ELI** rushes to another table and has someone there help him read the review [using their mad-lib answers]. **ABIGAIL** and **TONY** have lowered their guns, everyone is listening to the review.)*

ABIGAIL. Now that's a review that pays the rent!

TOFFEE. I think we really hit it BIG!

(Everyone cheers.)

BAXTER. *(to audience)* And that's when Bernie decided to stagger back in and fall against the light switches – killing the lights.

*(Lights out. Sound of a struggle between **TOFFEE** and **MIMI** and **TONY** and **BERNIE**.)*

MIMI. Bernie, you little two faced –

TOFFEE. If I get my hands on you, I'm gonna kill you –

BERNIE. Hey, I know it's dark, but don't you think we should get a private room before we pull each others clothes off? –

ELI. Don't you dare – or I'll – I'll –

TONY. Hey, give me back my gun.

BAXTER. Let me show you what we really mean by making a hit on Broadway.

*(Two gunshots. Spotlights up. **BAXTER** side steps into the light.)*

BAXTER. Hi. Ah – well – it seems that in the dark someone plugged our investor – with his own gun.

(Lights up. **TONY** *drops dead.* **ELI** *holds up the gun.)*

ABIGAIL. Oh – Eli!

(Lights out. Music.)

Intermission

Scene Three

(Lights out. Music "YOU" begins to play. Spotlight up on **ABIGAIL.** **MIMI**, **TOFFEE**, **BERNIE**, **ELI**, *and* **BAXTER** *are spread out around the room as* **ABIGAIL**, *now wearing her badge, paces about, singing and accusing each of them.)*

ABIGAIL.

YOU
ALL HAD A MOTIVE TO
SHOOT A FEW SLUGS THROUGH
TONY, THE GANG-STER, SOMEONE WE ALL KNEW

ITS TRUE
HAD TO BE ONE OF YOU
TOOK THE MOMENT TO
GRAB HIS GUN AND PLUG HIM THROUGH AND THROUGH

(Starts to rumba. **ELI** *joins her rumba line, as does everyone else)*

NOW HE'S DEAD
CAN'T – TESTIFY
NOW MY CASE
NOT – CUT AND DRY
NOW I'M FACED
WITH – HOMICIDE
HAVE TO FIND OUT WHO

KNEW THIS SHOW
JUST – CLEVER WAY
LAUNDER CASH
PROOF – CAME TODAY
ALL OF YOU
INNOCENT YOU SAY
SHOW IS SUDDENLY A HIT

BUT STILL
TONY GOT HIS FILL
NOW HE'S IN THE CHILL
ONE OF YOU WILL HAVE TO PAY THE BILL

ALL.

> BUT STILL
> TONY GOT HIS FILL
> NOW HE'S IN THE CHILL
> ONE OF US WILL HAVE TO PAY THE BILL
>
> *(music under)*

MIMI. Wait a second. Eli was the one holding the gun when the lights came back on!

BERNIE. Yeah!

TOFFEE. Yeah!

ELI. Yeah! – *(confused)* So?

BAXTER. Oh, come on. None of you could really think that our own Eli Blaine – could possibly have pulled the trigger on big bad Tony Alto?

> *(They all look at* **ELI.***)*

TOFFEE. Well, Tony did threaten the woman he loves.

> *(They all look at* **ABIGAIL.** *She's shocked.)*

ABIGAIL. *(sighing)* Oh, Eli.

> *(music back up)*

ELI.

> WHY
> JUST WHEN-EVER I TRY
> LOOK HER RIGHT IN THE EYE
> I GET JUST A SYMPATHETIC SIGH
>
> MAY-BE
> WHEN YOU ALL LAUGH AT ME
> THERE'S SOMETHING YOU DON'T SEE
> THE CALCULATED KILLER I COULD BE

ABIGAIL. Is this a confession, Eli?

ELI. Do I get handcuffed to you?

BERNIE. Sounds like a confession to me. Case closed. Lets go home. Or at least to another bar.

BAXTER. Eli, how many times did you shoot Tony Alto?

ELI. Ten.

ABIGAIL. His revolver only holds six bullets.

ELI. I meant six.

ABIGAIL. And there were four left in the gun.

ELI. Four.

MIMI & TOFFEE & BERNIE. He meant two.

(music up again)

TOFFEE.
> TON-Y
> WAS AS BAD AS COULD BE
> FEARED BY ALL THAT HE'D SEE
> FROM HIM NO ONE COULD EVER SAFELY FLEE

ALL.
> BUT STILL
> TONY GOT HIS FILL
> NOW HE'S IN THE CHILL
> ONE OF YOU WILL HAVE TO PAY THE BILL

MIMI. It's little Ms. Toffee Alto that first accused Eli.

TOFFEE. No, you pointed out he was holding the gun.

BERNIE. Actually, I'm rather disappointed. I expected you two be accusing each other – sparks flying – hair pulling – Ohhh –

TOFFEE & MIMI. Oh, shut up.

BAXTER. Let's face it, we all had a motive.

MIMI. I most certainly did not.

BERNIE. Ha!

ALL.
> BUT STILL
> TONY GOT HIS FILL
> NOW HE'S IN THE CHILL
> ONE OF US WILL HAVE TO PAY THE BILL
> HAVE
> TO
> PAY
> THE
> BILL

(Lights out. Spotlight up on **BAXTER.** *)*

BAXTER. *(to audience)* Okay, so maybe it wasn't exactly like that. But I am a musical producer – we tend to exaggerate. Suffice it to say, our best chorus girl turned out to be an undercover FBI agent and she was determined to find out who had killed our backer, Tony Alto. Honestly, I'm sure nobody else cared.

(lights up)

ABIGAIL. Eli, how did you end up holding the murder weapon?

ELI. I didn't know it was the murder weapon.

MIMI. Oh, God – You're almost as stupid as your play.

BAXTER. How dare you say that in front of our esteemed director. *(placing hand on audience member shoulder)* who said this was by far their proudest work – and let's not forget he *(or she)* was the director on such spectacular productions as *Stinking in the Rain, Kick Me Kate* and *The Texas Chainsaw Musical.*

MIMI. I invested in that last one. Eli, where's that gun?

*(***ELI*** *starts to look for the gun.* **ABIGAIL** *stops him.)*

BAXTER. Wait a second. I speak playwright. *(with exaggerated hand motions)* Eli, how did you end up with Tony Alto's gun?

ELI. Ohhh, *(with exaggerated hand motions)* Someone handed it to me in the dark.

ABIGAIL. Who?

ELI. I don't know, it was dark. I heard the shots and then someone just shoved something into my hands. When the lights came on, I was holding a gun. Hey – that's a great way to start a play. "Gun Shy in the Dark!" *(to audience member)* Can I borrow your napkin? Does anyone have a pencil?

BAXTER. Make sure it's a musical!

MIMI. Oh, for the sake of humanity – don't.

ABIGAIL. In the dark, who was standing near you?

ELI. I don't know. It was dark.

(Everyone sighs, frustrated.)

TOFFEE. He was right next to Tony when Bernie fell into the light switches and knocked them out.

BERNIE. Hey – you mean, I can say I knocked Tony Alto's lights out?

MIMI. You can say you did more than that. You can say you knocked Tony's Altos wife –

TOFFEE. *(quickly interrupting)* Tony had his gun on you and was going to shoot you, Abigail. He hated the FBI – especially women FBI agents. Once my son was watching that show, *X-Files*, and Tony walked into the room and blew the whole set away. If Eli hadn't wrestled the gun away from Tony in the dark, you would be dead.

ELI. Huh?

TOFFEE. You're her hero, Eli – saving Abigail's life like that.

ELI. I am? Wow – I am!

MIMI. He saved your life too, then, didn't he little miss Mafia Queen?

TOFFEE. Eli's everyone's hero.

MIMI. Especially since you wanted Tony out of the way. You thought Bernie was going to shack up with you. But how does a mafia queen divorce the mafia – seeing that you're Catholic? Only one way and that's with bullets. Go on, tell our FBI agent all about it, Bernie.

BERNIE. Nonsense. Besides, I would never implicate the woman I love!

*(**BERNIE** goes to **TOFFEE** and holds her hands.)*

I'll be right beside you in these hard times.

MIMI. She wants you bed-side, Bernie. But just remember, her money's gonna be tied up for a long time now that the piggy bank is dead and the feds will be looking into where every penny game from. Right, Abigail?

ABIGAIL. Standard procedure is to freeze assets of anyone brought up on charges of money laundering – and their spouse.

BERNIE. Oh, my poor, darling Toffee. *(kisses her, turns to* **ABIGAIL***)* She hated Tony. Couldn't wait to be rid of him.

*(***TOFFEE*** starts hitting ***BERNIE***. ***BERNIE*** screams and runs into ***MIMI****'s arms.)*

MIMI. He always comes back to Mimi.

TOFFEE. He was going to kill you, Bernie. Someone told him you was giving me more than acting lessons and he came into that back room gunning for you. That's why you shot him. You grabbed the gun from me in the dark.

BERNIE. No, I didn't. I grabbed the gun from Tony, I think. You grabbed the gun from me.

ELI. I grabbed the gun from Tony.

(They all look at **ELI***.)*

I did! He was aiming it at Abigail. *(sighs)* Abigail. Don't you just saying that?

BAXTER. We've been through that already, Eli. Never reuse your own material.

ABIGAIL. Eli, you really took the gun away from Tony Alto?

ELI. Of course I did. I had too.

ABIGAIL. *(sweetly)* Oh, Eli! Why – that was really sweet.

ELI. *(smiling at her)* I was hoping you'd think so.

MIMI. This is as bad as the love scene in your play. "You shot him, for me?"

(She does a gagging gesture – sticks her finger in her mouth. But she's holding an olive on her stirring stick and it gets stuck in her throat. She gags but no one realizes it's for real.)

TOFFEE. We get the point, Mimi. You didn't like the scene. But you don't have to be so gross about it. I thought the scene was just wonderful, Eli. Didn't you Bernie?

BERNIE. Actually – I thought it was one of the most moving moments of the play. Of musical theater in fact.

BAXTER. It was inspired genus, Eli.

ELI. Gosh, thanks.

*(**MIMI** has been pointing to her throat, that she's gagging for real.)*

ABIGAIL. Eli, – how can I put this? Did you –

*(Everyone looks at the still gagging **MIMI**, who has staggered around the room and is now next to **ELI**. He thinks she's clowning.)*

ELI. No wonder your column is so popular, Ms. Sheraton. You sure are funny.

*(He slaps her on the back, turning away. This dislodges the olive choking **MIMI**, who swallows.)*

Anyway, someone grabbed the gun away from me in the dark.

BAXTER. I grabbed the gun from you, Eli.

*(Everyone stares at **BAXTER**.)*

Well – there's nothing more dangerous than a playwright with a gun in a room full of actors. But someone grabbed the gun from me. I think it was Mimi. It smelled like her.

MIMI. You would recognize my perfume in the dark?

BAXTER. Sure – double martini.

MIMI. Don't mind if I do. Bernie!

*(She raises her glass. **BERNIE** fetches it and goes to the bar.)*

ABIGAIL. Mimi, when you said you didn't have a motive, Bernie laughed. Why?

MIMI. *(pointing to audience member)* He hear this man whispering something to his date.

*(**BERNIE** brings the glass back to **MIMI**. Looks at the man and laughs – then stops abruptly when **MIMI** glares at him.)*

BAXTER. Mimi, how's your cash flow?

MIMI. I make a nice sum for my column, thank you very much. It's syndicated and widely read – which means this show is dead.

(She downs her drink, looks at the olive. She feeds it to **BERNIE.** *)*

ELI. Abigail or Annie, or – what should I call you?

ABIGAIL. Anything you like.

ELI. Darling, I don't understand something. This money laundering? Where did Mr. Alto get the money he needed to launder?

ABIGAIL. Did you just call me – ah – Tony Alto made money from illegal gambling, loan sharking, sale of stolen merchandise, prostitution.

BAXTER. *(to* **MIMI** *)* So which one are you?

BERNIE. Three out of four, I'd say.

MIMI. Bernie, shut up.

TOFFEE. *(realizing it)* She owes him money! She owed Tony money! Tony told me not to worry about the show getting good reviews, 'cause he had a newspaper woman who was in deep!

BAXTER. And Bernie always goes where the money is, which explains why you couldn't hold on to him any more. And why Toffee Alto was such an attractive package. Just Bernie's type – loaded.

BERNIE. And frustrated. *(to a woman in the audience)* And you look both tonight, darling. Maybe I can help.

MIMI. I should have let him plug you.

TOFFEE. *(jumping up and down with joy)* Mimi had a motive, Mimi had a motive!

MIMI. *(imitating* **TOFFEE** *)* So did Baxter. So did Baxter.

ELI. Baxter? Nooo. Baxter could never harm anyone. There's not a single mean bone in his body.

MIMI. He's a producer – there's not a single bone in his body. They're snakes. And if by some miracle the show ever started selling tickets, Baxter wouldn't see a cent. He would just keep getting a small pay out to keep the thing up. But with these sudden good reviews, God knows there's no accounting for taste, this front could really take off. And that would leave Baxter out in the cold.

ELI. I'd give him my sweater.

BAXTER. Thanks, Eli.

ELI. Don't mention it, Baxter.

ABIGAIL. Once the feds found out this show was a money laundering operation, we'd close it down. But if Tony were dead, we might drop the case. That's what you were hoping for, wasn't Baxter?

ELI. None of those thoughts ever entered his mind. He doesn't need Tony Alto – not when he has a partner like Eli Blaine – and stars like Toffee Alto and Bernie Broadhurst. Sure, he was riding on easy street. But things had been tough before and, in the theater business, that's a natural state of being. We made a hit, we can make another one – and this time with the kind and eager investments of people who know and love theater – who recognize a good thing when they see it – who believe that a good opening night party is worth the price of their investment, because in all probability that's the only thing besides house seats they'll ever see of their money. I just know that some people in this room would give anything to invest in Baxter Mallenstock, the best producer, the best partner, the best friend.

BAXTER. *(touched)* Oh, Eli – I – I – for once in my life – I really don't know what to say.

ELI. Don't say anything, just listen to the latest review!

(**ELI** *goes to a table and helps them read a review.* **BERNIE** *picks up the cigar left by* **TONY.**)

BERNIE. I think you were ahead before you went to the reviews, Eli.

(**BERNIE** *puts the cigar in his mouth.*)

ELI. Well, a lot of shows make it, despite mixed reviews. Don't they?

(Spotlight on **BAXTER**. *Lights down.)*

BAXTER. It was at that moment that, for the first time, I realized why I ever wanted to become a theatrical producer. It wasn't for the women, and money, and the fame – oh, who am I fooling. Of course it was for the women and the money and the fame. But it was also because I wanted someone to see me for more than what I had always been – which was a loser. And Eli Blaine – Eli Blaine did. *(Pause, he wipes his eyes.)* Excuse me, I'm not used to emotion – I'm a Broadway producer. But, am I a murderer? I need you folks to help me out. I've told you what happened. Now you tell me – and Agent Annie Abigail Muller – who do you think is the killer.

(Lights out. Cast mingles, implicate each other and collect sleuth sheets.)

*(***TOFFEE*** implicates* **MIMI & ELI**.*)*

*(***MIMI*** implicates* **BAXTER & TOFFEE**.*)*

*(***BERNIE*** implicates* **TOFFEE & BAXTER**.*)*

*(***ELI*** implicates* **MIMI**.*)*

*(***BAXTER*** defends* **ELI**.*)*

*(***ABIGAIL*** asks everyone who they think did it and why.)*

Scene Four
FINALE

(Music. Lights up. Everyone is at the bar, except **ABIGAIL** *who is approached by* **BERNIE.***)*

BERNIE. So, Agent Abigail or Annie, or – whatever. Do you think you know who killed Tony Alto?

ABIGAIL. Sure. It was easy. It was the person who had the most to gain from his death. Usually is.

BERNIE. Oh – I guess that would be Baxter then?

*(***BAXTER** *joins them, hearing his name.)*

BAXTER. Someone mention my name – in a derogatory way I hope.

BERNIE. Just discussing why Agent Abigail is going to arrest you for Tony Alto's murder.

ABIGAIL. What would he have to gain? If Tony Alto were dead, that would dry up his funding to keep this show up. We were in it, we know he couldn't rely on ticket sales. Now it'll have to close.

BERNIE. Oh – then I guess it was his wife, Toffee.

*(***ELI** *joins them.)*

ABIGAIL. Well, there's no doubt Toffee wanted him dead – but what woman wouldn't? The guy was a leech. But would she shoot him?

ELI. Sure – wouldn't she?

ABIGAIL. I doubt it. He was part of the family and that kind of family can be very vengeful. She may have wanted to be rid of the guy, but not at the expense of her own life. Nawh, it wasn't Toffee Alto.

BAXTER. Then Mimi. She owed him money.

BERNIE. And she wanted me back.

ABIGAIL. *(laugh)* Oh, you actors are so conceited. Bernie, Mimi could always get you back, whenever she wanted to. All she'd have to do is snap her fingers and you'd be by her side, with a fresh martini. You two are two of kind and besides each other, no one else would ever put up with either of you for long. As far as her debts are concerned – maybe. But Mimi kills with the pen, not the sword. Nawh, it wasn't Mimi – unless she shot the wrong person in the dark.

ELI. Yeah! Maybe she was trying for Bernie and in the dark shot the wrong one!

ABIGAIL. Mimi is a woman who keeps her emotions all bottled up inside. Push the wrong button and she's liable to explode – and Bernie would be the person she would explode on. But, if that were the case, she wouldn't have called Bernie back to her side like she just did. She's not a woman who holds a grudge. Nawh – I still say, not Mimi.

BERNIE. Eli?

ELI. Me?

ABIGAIL. *(smiling at him)* Eli. He's really genuinely sweet, isn't he?

(He smiles back.)

BERNIE. He said he pulled the gun from Tony's hands. Eli could have shot Tony, to defend you?

ABIGAIL. You know, I almost believe he could have. Except someone like Eli wouldn't know the first thing about guns. And in the dark – well, Eli would be too nervous to even figure out which direction to aim the thing.

ELI. That's true.

ABIGAIL. But it's the thought that counts.

(They exchange smiles.)

BERNIE. But that leaves only me. You can't think I killed Tony Alto? I mean, lets face it, I'm a wimp. I'd rather run than fight.

ABIGAIL. That's very true. No – I'm sure Bernie Broadhurst didn't shoot Tony Alto either. He simply wouldn't have the guts.

ELI. I don't get it. That was everyone, wasn't it?

ABIGAIL. No. No one's mentioned the person who would benefit the most from Tony Alto's death.

ELI & BAXTER & BERNIE. Who?

ABIGAIL. Tony Alto – of course.

ELI. He killed himself?

ABIGAIL. He tried. Tonight not only did we have enough to convict him on money laundering but murder as well.

BAXTER. The corpse in the men's room?

ABIGAIL. Our missing State witness. We picked up one of Tony's stooges, who claims Tony told him to shoot the guy and leave him in the bathroom. He didn't know why, but he wasn't about to disobey Tony Alto.

BERNIE. He would never have testified against Tony Alto.

ABIGAIL. Of course he would. Witness relocation. Besides, nobody who worked for Tony liked him in the least.

BERNIE. What? Come on, I'm sure they must have.

(TOFFEE walks up to BERNIE, who has the cigar, and slaps him. He gets ready to punch her back, but stops himself as she lectures him.)

BERNIE. What's that for?

TOFFEE. Always running back to Mimi. I told her she can keep you. Why, you're almost as bad as that two-timing degenerate husband of mine. At least I got to cheat on him once before he bought the bullet. It still don't make up for the three dozen or so he's had. That morta de – er – bum. I was sorry I married him from the first day of the honeymoon. But not no more. Now I get the bank and the insurance – the feds can't take that away.

BERNIE. I thought you loved him?

TOFFEE. Ha! I tolerated him. No one loves a wise guy, not even their own mother. I'll tell yeah, the only people showing up at his funeral will be those who just want to make sure that gumba – er – bum is dead.

(BERNIE starts to get angry. MIMI joins them with The New York Times *and* Variety *– and her martini.)*

MIMI. Hold everything! He's finally out – and I'm not talking about you, darling *(she pats a man on the shoulder)*. The definitive in theater reviewer – the paper that tells you if you're a hit, or closing in one night. *The New York Times.* Drum roll, Bernie.

BERNIE. *(angry, cigar in his mouth)* What?

MIMI. *(rolling her eyes)* I'll do it myself.

> **(MIMI** *takes* The New York Times *to a table – it stinks as well.)*

BAXTER. Well, if we weren't sunk before, now we're really down the tank.

MIMI. *(holding out glass)* Justice has been served. Bernie – martini.

BERNIE. *(angry)* What?

MIMI. Hop to it, Bernie dear. I'm dry and it's your job to keep me moist.

BERNIE. Get it yourself.

MIMI. Bernie – what on earth is the matter with you? Why aren't you behaving?

ABIGAIL. Because that's not Bernie. That's Tony Alto.

ALL. Tony Alto?

ABIGAIL. When Tony came in with his gun drawn he said he had it all figured out. What he had figured out was how to get away before I could arrest him. In the dark he took the opportunity to plug Bernie and pretend to be him. It only had to be for the rest of the night, just long enough to get away and out of town before we did an autopsy on the corpse and checked its fingerprints. It was the cigar that gave you away. Bernie hated cigars – he even took one away from Baxter earlier this evening. Tony Alto, you're under arrest.

> *(***TONY*** *smiles. They both pull guns at the same time.)*

MIMI. Another gun? What, are you a walking Wal-Marts?

TONY/BERNIE. Shut up – all of you.

> *(He points the gun at* **ELI**.*)*

TONY. Hand over your gun, Agent Abigail, or the putz gets it.

ELI. Putz?

(**ABIGAIL** *hands* **TONY** *her gun.*)

ABIGAIL. You'll never get away, Tony. This room is filled with undercover agents.

(*The waiters all pull out guns.* **TONY** *points his gun at* **ABIGAIL.**)

TONY. All I need is a hostage.

(*As he approaches her,* **ELI** *steps in his way.*)

ELI. Take me.

TONY. Alright – I'll take the both of you.

(**BAXTER** *joins them.*)

BAXTER. And me too. After all, we're partners.

TONY. What? What am I gonna do with three freakin hostages?

TOFFEE. You never knew what to do – especially in the bedroom – which is why you went through so many mistresses. They kept getting bored.

TONY. (*turning gun on* **TOFFEE**) I've had about all I can take from you.

(**MIMI** *comes up to him with a martini.*)

MIMI. Well, before you go – have one on the house.

(*She throws the drink in his face and grabs his gun.*)

(*scream*) Now what do I do with it?

(**TONY** *pulls out the gun he took from* **ABIGAIL.**)

TOFFEE. Shoot him!

(**MIMI** *shoots –* **TONY**'*s foot. Then she hands the gun to* **TOFFEE.**)

MIMI. That was for Bernie.

(**TONY** *turns the gun towards* **TOFFEE,** *who shoots him – in the crotch.*)

TOFFEE. And that's for all your mistresses.

> (*She hands the gun to* **BAXTER**. *He points the gun at* **TONY**.)

BAXTER. Sorry, can't think of anything.

> (*hands gun to* **ELI**)

ELI. Me neither!

> (*Hands gun to* **ABIGAIL**. **TONY** *bolts out the front door.*)

ABIGAIL. Let him have it boys – he's a lousy tipper.

> (*The waiters all shoot out the door as they exit after him.* **ABIGAIL** *crosses to doorway and looks out.*)

ABIGAIL. Boy, they got him good. Well, I guess that closes the case. Mimi, I'm sorry about Bernie.

MIMI. (*cries*) Bernie! (*stops crying instantly as she looks at a man in the audience*) Well, there's always more where he came from. (*to man*) Tell me, do you know how to make a dry martini? First you get it wet and then – well, I'll teach you.

> (*She growls at the man in the audience.*)

ELI. But shouldn't we have a big Broadway ending?

> (*Music starts to "Broadway"*)

I'M A PLAYWRIGHT, BUT NOT FORMER
I SOLD HOTDOGS ON THE CORNER
AS A VENDOR ON WEST 42ND STREET
THEN I MET A MAN NAMED BAXTER
WHO BECAME MY BENEFACTOR
HAD ME WRITE A SHOW AND HE FILLED EVERY SEAT

BAXTER.
WE'LL PUT ON A SHOW TOGETHER
AND WE'LL BE PARTNERS FOREVER
I'LL TAKE ANY CHECK WE SNAG DOWN TO THE BANK
I'LL SPEND ALL OUR HARD EARNED MONEY
GET AN OFFICE, A BLOND HONEY
WE JUST HOPE THE SHOW DON'T END UP DOWN THE TANK

ALL.

> BROADWAY
> BROADWAY
> SEE THE LIGHTS
> MEET ALL TYPES
> ON BROADWAY
>
> BROADWAY
> BROADWAY
> ALL THE FOLKS
> HAVE HIGH HOPES
> ON BROADWAY

TOFFEE.

> I WAS JUST A GIRL FROM JERSEY
> WITH A GANGSTER THRU THE CLERGY
> TIL ELI AND BAXTER PUT ME IN THEIR SHOW
> NOW MY GANGSTER'S SIX FEET UNDER
> AND BROADWAY HAS WET MY HUNGER
> I'LL HELP FINANCE THEIR NEXT SHOW WITH TONY'S
>   DOUGH

> *(music under)*

ELI. You will?

TOFFEE. If you write me a great part!

BAXTER. Of course he will! He's Eli Blaine!

> *(The all shake hands. **ELI** turns to **ABIGAIL**. Music up)*

ABIGAIL.

> FBI WORK WAS NEVER
> AS MUCH FUN AS THIS

ALL.

> BEING IN A BIG BROADWAY SHOW

ABIGAIL.

> NEVER KNOW WHO YOU'LL MEET,
> GUY LIKE ELI, SO SWEET

ALL.

> BY BEING IN A BIG BROADWAY SHOW

MIMI.

OH I THINK I'LL BE SICK,
NEED A MARTINI QUICK
MUST SIT THRU ANOTHER BAD SHOW

ALL.

WE'LL ALL HAVE GOOD SEATS
THE NEXT TIME THAT WE MEET
AT THE OPENING OF THEIR NEXT BROADWAY SHOW!

(Music under, spot on **BAXTER**, *lights out.)*

BAXTER. Well, that's what happened on my way from the Forum theater, where our show *The Mafia Queen* opened and closed on the same night. But Toffee Alto has already put up the front money for our new venture "Gun Shy in the Dark." Abigail gave Eli her number and I – well, I got not only a good partner, but a good friend. So, why was I arrested? I stiffed the restaurant where we had the party. Hey, I'm a Broadway producer – some habits are hard to break.

(Lights out, music up. Cast bow during music. Waiters bow. Award prizes, play music out as cast exits.)

BROADWAY MUSICAL SHOW TITLES IN SCRIPT
(36)

42nd street

Beauty and the Beast

Dreamgirls

Cabaret

Crazy for You

Le Miserable

Oklahoma

Sound of Music

Nine

Footlose

Carousel

Peter Pan

Annie Get Your Gun

Jekyll & Hyde

Grand Hotel

Stop the world I Want to get off

Sweet Charity

Big

Rocky Horror Show

Chicago

Chorus line

Gypsy

Grease

My One and Only

Most Happy Fellow

Saturday Night Fever

Titanic

Scarlet Pimpernel

Cats

Annie

She Loves Me

Bandwagon

Promises, Promises

I Do, I Do

Rent

Jersey Boys

PROPS

Cash, ones & hundreds, for Baxter

Cigar

5 Newspapers (with the mad-libs reviews pasted inside)

Martini glass & olives for Mimi

Cocktail glasses (five)

4 Blonde wigs

2 pair White opera gloves

4 White minks

Thug's leather jacket, baseball cap, sunglasses

Thug's gun

Abigail' s gun

Badge for Abigail

Tony's gun

Guns for waiters

MAD-LIBS

1
THE RECORD

Broadway has a new ____________ tonight, with the opening of *the Mafia Queen*. Producer Baxter Mallenstock has mounted a _________ of a show, With songs like a _______ and story right out of __________, the Mafia Queen is sure to be the next __________ of theater history.

2
THE POST

The Mafia Queen took New York by ____________ tonight. It looks like producer Baxter Mallenstock and Playwright Eli Blaine have struck ___________ with a show that gives audiences a _________ for their money. New Star Toffee Alto is a true _______ and Bernard Broadhurst proves why he's known as the _______ of Broadway.

3
THE NEWS

The Forum theater on Broadway was host to a _________ tonight. *The Mafia Queen* proves that Broadway isn't _________ but __________. With such a _______ of talent, this show is sure to become the __________ of the Great White Way.

4
THE LEDGER

Watch out Broadway, there's a new _______ in town, called *The Mafia Queen*. You could just see the _______ of a show yourself, or you could just have a ________! If __________ is your cup of tea, than the Mafia Queen is the __________ for you.

5
THE NEW YORK TIMES

What can one say about *The Mafia Queen*, the new _____ that ________ Broadway tonight, spreading _________ across the great white way. The show is moving – to ___________ hopefully. No amount of _________ will help this _______ stay afloat.

REVIEWS

1
WE NEED YOU TO
HELP WRITE A REVIEW!

Here's all you have to do. Fill in an appropriate word in the blanks provided. Please keep it "PG." Later this evening, someone at your table will be asked to stand up and read out the words one at a time, filling in the blanks in a review! It's fun and easy.

THE RECORD

(Fairy Tale Character) _______________________

(Animal) _____________________

(Type of bird)_____________________

(TV Show) _________________

(Famous Event) ________________

2
WE NEED YOU TO
HELP WRITE A REVIEW!

Here's all you have to do. Fill in an appropriate word in the blanks provided. Please keep it "PG." Later this evening, someone at your table will be asked to stand up and read out the words one at a time, filling in the blanks in a review! It's fun and easy.

THE NEWS

(Weather Condition) _______________

(Mineral/gem) _________________

(Sports term) _______________

(Make of car) ________________

(Cartoon Character) _______________

3
WE NEED YOU TO
HELP WRITE A REVIEW!

Here's all you have to do. Fill in an appropriate word in the blanks provided. Please keep it "PG." Later this evening, someone at your table will be asked to stand up and read out the words one at a time, filling in the blanks in a review! It's fun and easy. (Natural disasters are such things as earthquakes, etc, ... Physical stae of beings are living, breathing suffering, etc.)

THE POST

(Natural disaster) ________________

(Physical state of being) _______________ing

(Physical Activity) _______________ing

(Unit of measure)________________

(Super hero) ________________

4

**WE NEED YOU TO
HELP WRITE A REVIEW!**

Here's all you have to do. Fill in an appropriate word in the blanks provided. Please keep it "PG." Later this evening, someone at your table will be asked to stand up and read out the words one at a time, filling in the blanks in a review! It's fun and easy.

THE LEDGER

(Mythical creature) _______________________

(Fast Food) _____________________

(Medical Operation)_____________________

(Kind of punishment)_________________________

(Medicine) _______________________________

5

**WE NEED YOU TO
HELP WRITE A REVIEW!**

Here's all you have to do. Fill in an appropriate word in the blanks provided. Please keep it "PG." Later this evening, someone at your table will be asked to stand up and read out the words one at a time, filling in the blanks in a review! It's fun and easy.

THE NY TIMES

(Name of Villain) _____________________

(Violent action) _______________ed

(Name of disease) ___________________

(Far off place) __________________

(Name of Drug) _________________

(Name of Fish) ___________________

Also by
David Landau...

The Altos

Contempt of Court

Murder at Cafe Noir

Murderous Crossing

Noir Point Blank

Noir Suspicions